Henry and Mudge and a Very Merry Christmas

The Twenty-Fifth Book of Their Adventures

Story by Cynthia Rylant
Pictures by Suçie Stevenson

READY-TO-READ

ALADDIN
New York   London   Toronto   Sydney

THE HENRY AND MUDGE BOOKS

ALADDIN PAPERBACKS
An imprint of Simon & Schuster Children's Publishing Division
1230 Avenue of the Americas, New York, NY 10020
Text copyright © 2004 by Cynthia Rylant
Illustrations copyright © 2004 by Suçie Stevenson
Also available in a Simon & Schuster Books for Young Readers hardcover edition.
Designed by Lucy Ruth Cummins
The text of this book was set in 18-point Goudy.
The illustrations were rendered in pen-and-ink and watercolor.
Manufactured in the United States of America
First Aladdin Paperbacks edition October 2005
10 9 8 7 6 5 4
ISBN-13: 978-0-689-81168-5 (hc.)
ISBN-10: 0-689-81168-3 (hc.)
ISBN-13: 978-0-689-83448-6 (pbk.)
ISBN-10: 0-689-83448-9 (pbk.)

Contents

Christmastime

Henry and Henry's big dog, Mudge,
loved Christmastime.
They loved the smells—cinnamon in the
kitchen, peppermint in the living room,
pine on the front door.

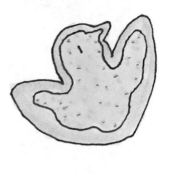

But the smell they loved most of all was the smell of cutout cookies.

This Christmas Henry's mother was making cutout cookies for all of the relatives: for Henry grandmother and for Great-Grandpa Bill.

For Aunt Sally and for Uncle Jake.

For Cousin Annie and for Uncle Ed.

The relatives were coming for Christmas breakfast, and they would all have cookies to take home.

7

Henry and Mudge went into the kitchen
to help.

Henry cut out birds for his grandmother and
houses for Great-Grandpa Bill.

He cut out hearts for Aunt Sally and trucks for Uncle Jake.

He cut out bunnies for Annie and books for Uncle Ed.

Mudge just licked the floor a lot.
"Mudge is a good helper," Henry told
his mother.
"He's licking the kitchen all clean."

"Hmmm," said Henry's mother with a smile.
"Maybe we should make Christmas cookies
in **your** room!"

Applause

On Christmas Eve, Henry was very happy.

There were presents under the tree.

Snow was falling.

Candles were glowing.

"I think we should go caroling," said
Henry's father.
"With Annie and Uncle Ed."
"Great idea!" said Henry.

Annie and Uncle Ed came over from next door.
Annie was wearing big white earmuffs and
carrying her white bunny, Snowball.

"It looks like you have bunnies on your head," said Henry.

Annie giggled.

16

Mudge sniffed Snowball.
Then Mudge sniffed the earmuffs just to
make sure.

"It's too cold to take Snowball," Annie said.
"I'll just let her play in your room."
(Snowball loved Henry's room. There were so
many piles of things to hide under.)
Annie put Snowball in Henry's room.

Then Henry and Mudge and Henry's parents
and Annie and Uncle Ed all went caroling.
It was fun.

They got cookies and hot chocolate
and applause.
They even got an old shoe.

When they went back to Henry's house,
they lit candles and ate gingerbread and talked

Snowball rode around the room on
Mudge's back.

Christmas was very near, and everyone was happy.

The Best Present

On Christmas morning, Annie and Uncle Ed
came over to open presents with Henry's family.

Annie got some new dresses and new lace hankies and new teacups for her collection. Henry got games and comics and two new fish (in his stocking!).

Mudge got a stuffed reindeer, and Snowball
got a coat.

"She's so **cute**!" said Annie.

Soon all of the relatives arrived for breakfast:
Grandma and Great-Grandpa Bill.
Aunt Sally.
Uncle Jake.
And the smell of pancakes filled the house.

Mudge and Snowball sat under the table while everyone ate.

A **lot** of food fell under the table.

Uncle Jake lost one whole pancake.
"Oops!" he said.

Aunt Sally lost one whole muffin.
"Oops!" she said.

Henry's father lost three slices of ham.
"Oops!" he said.

Mudge was very happy.

After breakfast the relatives went home with
their Christmas cookies.

Great-Grandpa Bill was biting off a chimney o
the way out the door.

When the house was quiet again, Henry helped
his parents clean up the kitchen.
(Mudge helped too, of course.)

Then they all went out for a walk.
They left seed bells in the trees for the birds.

They left walnuts on the ground for the squirrels.

They left cracked corn for the deer.

When they got back home, Henry put his arm
around Mudge.

"Merry Christmas, Mudge," Henry said.

"You're still the best present of all."

Mudge wagged and wagged and wagged.